THE MINTAGE

MORE WILDSIDE CLASSICS

The Nabob, by Alphonse Daudet
Out of the Wreck, by Captain A. E. Dingle
The Elm-Tree on the Mall, by Anatole France
The Lance of Kanana, by Harry W. French
Amazon Nights, by Arthur O. Friel
Caught in the Net, by Emile Gaboriau
The Gentle Grafter, by O. Henry
Raffles, by E. W. Hornung
Gates of Empire, by Robert E. Howard
Tom Brown's School Days, by Thomas Hughes
The Opium Ship, by H. Bedford Jones
The Miracles of Antichrist, by Selma Lagerlof
Arsène Lupin, by Maurice LeBlanc
A Phantom Lover, by Vernon Lee
The Iron Heel, by Jack London
The Witness for the Defence, by A.E.W. Mason
The Spider Strain and Other Tales, by Johnston McCulley
Tales of Thubway Tham, by Johnston McCulley
The Prince of Graustark, by George McCutcheon
Bull-Dog Drummond, by Cyril McNeile
The Moon Pool, by A. Merritt
The Red House Mystery, by A. A. Milne
Blix, by Frank Norris
Wings over Tomorrow, by Philip Francis Nowlan
The Devil's Paw, by E. Phillips Oppenheim
Satan's Daughter and Other Tales, by E. Hoffmann Price
The Insidious Dr. Fu Manchu, by Sax Rohmer
Mauprat, by George Sand
The Slayer and Other Tales, by H. de Vere Stacpoole
Penrod, by Booth Tarkington
The Gilded Age, by Mark Twain
The Blockade Runners, by Jules Verne
The Gadfly, by E.L. Voynich

Please see www.wildsidepress.com for a complete list!

THE MINTAGE

ELBERT HUBBARD

WILDSIDE PRESS

THE MINTAGE

This edition published 2005 by Wildside Press, LLC.
www.wildsidepress.com

CONTENTS

All success consists in this: you are doing something for somebody — are benefiting humanity; and the feeling of success comes from the consciousness of this.

FIVE BABIES

Riding on the Grand Trunk Railway a few weeks ago, going from Suspension Bridge to Chicago, I saw a sight so trivial that it seems unworthy of mention. Yet for three weeks I have remembered it, and so now I'll relate it, in order to get rid of it.

And possibly these little incidents of life are the items that make or mar existence.

But here is what I saw on that railroad train: five children, the oldest a girl of ten, and the youngest a baby boy of three. They were traveling alone and had come from Germany, duly tagged, ticketed and certified.

They were going to their Grandmother at Wau-kegan, Illinois.

The old lady was to meet them in Chicago.

The children spoke not a word of English, but there is a universal language of the heart that speaks and is understood. So the trainmen and the children were on very chummy terms.

Now, at London, Ontario, our train waited an hour for the Toronto and Montreal connections.

Just before we reached London, I saw the Conductor take the three smallest little passengers to the washroom at the end of the car, roll up their sleeves, turn their collars in, and duly wash their hands and faces. Then he combed their hair. They accepted the situation as if they belonged to the Conductor's family, as of course they did for the time being. It was a domestic scene that caused the whole car to smile, and made everybody know everybody else. A touch of nature makes a whole coach kin.

The children had a bushel-basket full of eatables, but at London that Conductor took the whole brood over to the dining-hall for supper, and I saw two fat men scrap as to who should have the privilege of paying for the kiddies' suppers. The children munched and smiled and said little things to each other in Teutonic whispers.

After our train left London and the Conductor had taken up his tickets, he came back, turned over two seats and placed the cushions lengthwise. One of the trainmen borrowed a couple of blankets from the sleeping-cars, and with the help of three volunteered overcoats, the babies were all put to bed, and duly tucked in.

I went back to my Pullman, and went to bed. And as I dozed off I kept wondering whether the Grandmother would be there in the morning to meet the little travelers. What sort of disaster had deprived them of parents, I did not know, nor did I care to ask. The children were alone, but among friends. They were strong and well, but they kept very close together and looked to the oldest girl as a mother.

But to be alone in Chicago would be terrible! Would she come!

And so I slept. In the morning there was another Conductor in charge, a man I had not before seen. I went into the day-coach, thinking that the man might not know about the babies, and that I might possibly help the little immigrants. But my services were not needed. The ten-year-old "little other mother" had freshened up her family, and the Conductor was assuring them, in awfully bad German, that their Grandmother would be there — although, of course, he didn't know anything at all about it.

When the train pulled into the long depot and stopped, the Conductor took the baby boy on one arm and a little girl on the other.

A porter carried the big lunch-basket, and the little other mother led a toddler on each side, dodging the hurrying passengers.

Evidently I was the only spectator of the play.

"Will she be there — will she be there?" I asked myself nervously.

She was there, all right, there at the gate. The Conductor was seemingly as gratified as I. He turned his charges over to the old woman, who was weeping for joy, and hugging the children between bursts of lavish, loving Deutsch.

I climbed into a Parmelee bus and said, "Auditorium Annex, please."

And as I sat there in the bus, while they were packing the grips on top, the Conductor passed by, carrying a tin box in one hand and his train cap in the other.

I saw an Elk's tooth on his watch-chain.

I called to him, "I saw you help the babies — good boy!"

He looked at me in doubt.

"Those German children," I said; "I'm glad you were so kind to them!"

"Oh," he answered, smiling; "yes, I had forgotten; why, of course, that is a railroad man's business, you know — to help everybody who needs help."

He waved his hand and disappeared up the stairway that led to the offices.

And it came to me that he had forgotten the incident so soon, simply because to help had become the habit of his life. He may read this, and he may not. There he was — big, bold, bluff and bronzed, his hair just touched with the frost of years, and beneath his brass buttons a heart beating with a desire to bless and benefit. I do not know his name, but the sight of the man, carrying a child on each arm, their arms encircling his neck in perfect faith, their long journey done, and he turning them over in safety to their Grandmother, was something to renew one's faith in humanity.

Even a great Railway System has a soul.

If you answer that corporations have no souls, I'll say: "Friend, you were never more mistaken in your life. The business that has no soul soon ceases to exist; and the success of a company or corporation turns on the kind of soul it possesses. Soul is necessary to service. Courtesy, kindness, honesty and efficiency are tangible soul-assets; and all good railroad men know it."

By taking thought you can add cubits to your stature.

TO THE WEST

To stand by the open grave of one you have loved, and feel the sky shut down over less worth in the world is the supreme test.

There you prove your worth, if ever.

You must live and face the day, and face each succeeding day, realizing that "the moving finger writes, and having writ moves on, nor all your tears shall blot a line of it."

Heroes are born, but it is calamity that discovers them.

Once in Western Kansas, in the early Eighties, I saw a loaded four-horse wagon skid and topple in going across a gully.

The driver sprang from his seat and tried to hold the wagon upright.

The weight was too great for his strength, powerful man though he was.

The horses swerved down the ditch instead of crossing it, and the overturning wagon caught the man and pinned him to the ground.

Half a dozen of us sprang from our horses. After

much effort the tangled animals were unhitched and the wagon was righted.

The man was dead.

In the wagon were the wife and six children, the oldest child a boy of fifteen. All were safely caught in the canvas top and escaped unhurt. We camped there — not knowing what else to do.

We straightened the mangled form of the dead, and covered the body with a blanket.

That night the mother and the oldest boy sat by the campfire and watched the long night away with their dead.

The stars marched in solemn procession across the sky.

The slow, crawling night passed.

The first faint flush of dawn appeared in the East.

I lay near the campfire, my head pillowed on a saddle, and heard the widowed mother and her boy talking in low but earnest tones.

"We must go back — we must go back to Illinois. It is the only thing to do," I heard the mother moan.

And the boy answered: "Mother, listen to what I say: We will go on — we will go on. We know where father was going to take us — we know what he was going to do. We will go on, and we will do what he intended to do, and if possible we will do it better. We will go on!"

That first burst of pink in the East had turned to gold.

Great streaks of light stretched from horizon to zenith.

I could see in the dim and hazy light the hobbled horses grazing across the plain a quarter of a mile away.

The boy of fifteen arose and put fuel on the fire.

After breakfast I saw that boy get a spade, a shovel and a pick out of the wagon.

With help of others a grave was dug there on the prairie.

The dead was rolled in a blanket and tied about with thongs, after the fashion of the Indians.

Lines were taken from a harness, and we lowered the body into the grave.

The grave was filled up by friendly hands working in nervous haste.

I saw the boy pat down the mound with the back of a spade.

I saw him carve with awkward, boyish hands the initials of his father, the date of his birth and the day of his death.

I saw him drive the slab down at the head of the grave.

I saw him harness the four horses.

I saw him help his little brothers into the canvas-covered wagon.

I saw him help his mother climb the wheel as she took her place on the seat.

I saw him spring up beside her.

I saw him gather up the lines in his brown, slim hands, and swing the whip over the leaders, as he gave the shrill word of command and turned the horses to the West.

And the cavalcade moved forward to the West —

always to the West.

The boy had met calamity and disaster. He had not flinched.

In a single day he had left boyhood behind and become a man.

And the years that followed proved him genuine.

What was it worked the change? Grief and responsibility, nobly met.

The church has aureoled and sainted the men and women who have fought the Cosmic Urge. To do nothing and to be nothing was regarded as a virtue.

SIMEON STYLITES
THE SYRIAN

As the traveler journeys through Southern Italy, Sicily and certain parts of what was Ancient Greece, he will see broken arches, parts of viaducts, and now and again a beautiful column pointing to the sky. All about is the desert, or solitary pastures, and only this white milestone marking the path of the centuries and telling in its own silent, solemn and impressive way of a day that is dead.

In the Fifth Century a monk called Simeon the Syrian, and known to us as Simeon Stylites, having taken the vow of chastity, poverty and obedience, began to fear greatly lest he might not be true to his pledge. And that he might live absolutely beyond reproach, always in public view, free from temptation, and free from the tongue of scandal, he decided to live in the world, and still not be of it. To this end he climbed to the top of a marble column, sixty feet high, and there on the capstone he began to live a life beyond reproach.

Simeon was then twenty-four years old.

The environment was circumscribed, but there were outlook, sunshine, ventilation — three good things. But beyond these the place had certain disadvantages. The capstone was a little less than three feet square, so Simeon could not lie down. He slept sitting, with his head bowed between his knees, and, indeed, in this posture he passed most of his time. Any recklessness in movement, and he would have slipped from his perilous position and been dashed to death upon the stones beneath.

As the sun arose he stood up, just for a few moments, and held out his arms in greeting, blessing and in prayer. Three times during the day did he thus stretch his cramped limbs, and pray with his face to the East. At such times, those who stood near shared in his prayers, and went away blessed and refreshed.

How did Simeon get to the top of the column?

Well, his companions at the monastery, a mile away, said he was carried there in the night by a miraculous power; that he went to sleep in his stone cell and awoke on the pillar. Other monks said that Simeon had gone to pay his respects to a fair lady, and in wrath God had caught him and placed him on high. The probabilities are, however, Terese, as viewed by an unbeliever, that he shot a line over the column with a bow and arrow and then drew up a rope ladder and ascended with ease.

However, in the morning the simple people of the scattered village saw the man on the column.

All day he stayed there.

And the next day he was still there.

The days passed, with the scorching heat of the midday sun, and the cool winds of the night.

Still Simeon kept his place.

The rainy season came on. When the nights were cold and dark, Simeon sat there with bowed head, and drew the folds of his single garment, a black robe, over his face.

Another season passed; the sun again grew warm, then hot, and the sandstorms raged and blew, when the people below almost lost sight of the man on the column. Some prophesied he would be blown off, but the morning light revealed his form, naked from the waist up, standing with hands outstretched to greet the rising sun.

Once each day, as darkness gathered, a monk came with a basket containing a bottle of goat's milk and a little loaf of black bread, and Simeon dropped down a rope and drew up the basket.

Simeon never spoke, for words are folly, and to the calls of saint or sinner he made no reply. He lived in a perpetual attitude of adoration.

Did he suffer? During those first weeks he must have suffered terribly and horribly. There was no respite nor rest from the hard surface of the rock, and aching muscles could find no change from the cramped and perilous position. If he fell, it was damnation for his soul — all were agreed as to this.

But man's body and mind accommodate themselves to almost any condition. One thing at least, Simeon was free from economic responsibilities, free from social cares and intrusion. Bores with sad stories of unappreciated lives and fond hopes unrealized, never broke in upon his peace. He was not pressed for time. No frivolous dame of tarnished fame sought to share with him his perilous perch. The people on a slow schedule, ten minutes late, never irritated his temper. His correspondence never got in a heap.

Simeon kept no track of the days, having no engagements to meet, nor offices to perform, beyond the prayers at morn, midday and night.

Memory died in him, the hurts became callouses, the world-pain died out of his heart, and to cling became a habit.

Language was lost in disuse.

The food he ate was minimum in quantity; sensation ceased, and the dry, hot winds reduced bodily tissue to a dessicated something called a saint — loved, feared and reverenced for his fortitude.

This pillar, which had once graced the portal of a pagan temple, again became a place of pious pilgrimage, and people flocked to Simeon's rock, so that they might be near when he stretched out his black, bony hands to the East, and the spirit of Almighty God, for a space, hovered close around.

So much attention did the abnegation of Simeon attract that various other pillars, marking the ruins of art and greatness gone, in that vicinity, were crowned with pious monks. The thought of these monks was to show how Christianity had triumphed over heathenism. Imitators were numerous. About then the Bishops in assembly asked, "Is Simeon sincere?" To test the matter of Simeon's pride, he was ordered to come down from his retreat.

As to his chastity, there was little doubt, his poverty was beyond question, but how about obedience to his superiors?

The order was shouted up to him in a Bishop's voice — he must let down his rope, draw up a ladder, and descend.

Straightway Simeon made preparation to obey. And then the Bishops relented and cried, "We have changed our minds, and now order you to remain!"

Simeon lifted his hands in adoration and thankfulness and renewed his lease.

And so he lived on and on and on — he lived on the top of that pillar, never once descending for thirty years.

All his former companions grew aweary, and one by one died, and the monastery bells tolled their requiem as they were laid to rest. Did Simeon hear the bells and say, "Soon it will be my turn"?

Probably not. His senses had flown, for what good were they! The young monk who now at eventide brought the basket with the bottle of goat's milk and the loaf of brown bread was born since Simeon had taken his place on the pillar.

"He has always been there," the people said, and crossed themselves hurriedly.

But one evening when the young monk came with his basket, no line was dropped down from above. He waited and then called aloud, but all in vain.

When sunrise came, there sat the monk, his face between his knees, the folds of his black robe drawn over his head. But he did not rise and lift his hands in prayer.

All day he sat there, motionless.

The people watched in whispered silence. Would he arise at sundown and pray, and with outstretched hands bless the assembled pilgrims?

And as they watched, a vulture came sailing slowly through the blue ether, and circled nearer and nearer; and off on the horizon was another — and still another, circling nearer and ever nearer.

I would write across the sky in letters of light this undisputed truth, proven by every annal of history, that the only way to help yourself is through loyalty to those who trust and employ you.

BATTLE OF THE LITTLE BIG HORN

It was in the Spring of Eighteen Hundred Seventy-six that the Sioux on the Dakota Reservation became restless, and after various fruitless efforts to restrain them, moved Westward in a body.

This periodic migration was a habit and a tradition of the tribe. For hundreds of years they had visited the buffalo country on an annual hunt.

Now the buffaloes were gone, save for a few scattered herds in the mountains. The Indians did not fully realize this, although they realized that as the Whites came in, the game went out. The Sioux were hunters and horsemen by nature. They traveled and moved about with great freedom. If restrained or interfered with they grew irritable and then hostile.

Now they were full of fight. The Whites had ruined the hunting-grounds; besides that, white soldiers had fought them if they moved to their old haunts, sacred for their use and bequeathed to them by their ancestors. In dead of Winter, when the snows lay deep and they were in their teepees, crouching around the scanty fire, soldiers had charged on horseback through the villages, shooting into the teepees, killing women and children.

At the head of these soldiers was a white chief, whom they called Yellow Hair. He was a smashing, dashing, fearless soldier who understood the Indian ways and haunts, and then used this knowledge for the undoing of the Red Men.

Yellow Hair wanted to keep them in one little place all the time, and desired that they should raise corn like cowardly Crows, when what they wanted was to be free and hunt!

They feared Yellow Hair — and hated him.

Custer was a man of intelligence — nervous, energetic, proud. His honesty and sincerity were beyond dispute. He was a natural Indian fighter. He could pull his belt one hole tighter and go three whole days without food. He could ride like the wind, or crawl in the grass, and knew how to strike, quickly and unexpectedly, as the first streak of dawn came into the East. Like Napoleon, he knew the value of time, and, in fact, he had somewhat of the dash and daring, not to mention the vanity, of the Corsican. His men believed in him and loved him, for he marched them to victory, and with odds of five to one had won again and again.

But Custer had the defect of his qualities; and to use the Lincoln phrase, sometimes took counsel of his ambition.

He had fought in the Civil War in places where no prisoners were taken, and where there was no commissary. And this wild, free life had bred in him a habit of unrest — a chafing at discipline and all rules of modern warfare.

Results were the only things he cared for, and power was his Deity.

When the Indians grew restless in the Spring of Seventy-six, Custer was called to Washington for consultation. President Grant was not satisfied with our Indian policy — he thought that in some ways the Whites were the real savages. The Indians he considered as children, not as criminals.

Custer tried to tell him differently. Custer knew the bloodthirsty character of the Sioux, their treachery and cunning — he showed scars by way of proof!

The authorities at Washington needed Custer. However, his view of the case did not mean theirs. Custer believed in the mailed hand, and if given the power he declared he would settle the Indian Question in America once and forever. His confidence and assumption and what Senator Dawes called swagger were not to their liking. Anyway, Custer was attracting altogether too much attention — the people followed him on Pennsylvania Avenue whenever he appeared.

General Terry was chosen to head the expedition against the hostile Sioux, and Custer was to go as second in command.

Terry was older than Custer, but Custer had seen more service on the plains. Custer demurred — threatened to resign — and wrote a note to the President asking for a personal interview and requesting a review of the situation.

President Grant refused to see Custer, and reminded him that the first duty of a soldier was obedience.

Custer left Washington, glum and sullen — grieved. But he was a soldier, and so he reported at Fort Lincoln, as ordered, to serve under a man who knew less about Indian fighting than did he.

The force of a thousand men embarked on six boats at Bismarck. There a banquet was given in honor of Terry and Custer. "You will hear from us by courier before July Fourth," said Custer.

He was still moody and depressed, but declared his willingness to do his duty.

Terry did not like his attitude and told him so. Poor Custer was stung by the reprimand.

He was only a boy, thirty-seven years old, to be sure, but with the whimsical, daring, ambitious and jealous quality of the center-rush. Custer at times had his eye on the White House — why not! Had not Grant been a soldier?

Women worshiped Custer, and men who knew him, never doubted his earnestness and honesty. He lacked humor.

He was both sincere and serious.

The expedition moved on up the tortuous Missouri, tying up at night to avoid the treacherous sandbars that lay in wait.

They had reached the Yellowstone River, and were getting into the Indian Country.

To lighten the boats, Terry divided his force into two parts. Custer disembarked on the morning of the Twenty-fifth of June, with four hundred forty-three men, besides a dozen who looked after the pack-train.

Scouts reported that the hostile Sioux were camped on the Little Big Horn, seventy-five miles across the country.

Terry gave Custer orders to march the seventy-five miles in forty-eight hours, and attack the Indians at the head of their camp at daylight on the morning of the Twenty-seventh. There was to be no parley — panic was the thing desired, and when Custer had started the savages on the run, Terry would attack them at the other end of their village, and the two fleeing mobs of savages would be driven on each other, and then they would cast down their arms and the trick would be done.

Next, to throw a cordon of soldiers around the camp and hold it would be easy.

Custer and his men rode away at about eight o'clock on the morning of the Twenty-fifth. They were in high spirits, for the cramped quarters on the transports made freedom doubly grateful.

They disappeared across the mesa and through the gray-brown hills, and soon only a cloud of dust marked their passage.

After five miles had been turned off on a walk, Custer ordered a trot, and then, where the ground was level, a canter.

On they went.

They pitched camp at four o'clock, having covered forty miles. The horses were unsaddled and fed, and supper cooked and eaten.

But sleep was not to be — these men shall sleep no more!

The bugles sounded "Boots and Saddles." Before sunset they were again on their way.

By three o'clock on the morning of the Twenty-sixth, they had covered more than seventy miles.

They halted for coffee.

The night, waiting for the dawn, was doubly dark.

Fast-riding scouts had gone on ahead, and now reported the Indians camped just over the ridge, four miles away.

Custer divided his force into two parts. The Indians were camped along the river for three miles. There were about two thousand of them, and the women and children were with them.

Reno with two hundred fifty men was ordered to swing around and attack the village from the South. Custer with one hundred ninety-three men would watch the charge, and when the valiant Reno had started the panic and the Indians were in confusion, his force would then sweep around and charge them from the other end of the village.

This was Terry's plan of battle, only Custer was going to make the capture without Terry's help.

When Terry came up the following day, he would find the work all done and neatly, too. Results are the only things that count, and victory justifies itself.

The battle would go down on the records as Custer's triumph!

Reno took a two-mile detour, and just at peep of day, ere the sun had gilded the tops of the cotton-woods, charged, with yells and rapid firing, into the Indian village. Custer stood on the ridge, his men mounted and impatient just below on the other side.

He could distinguish Reno's soldiers as they charged into the underbrush. Their shouts and the sound of firing filled his fighter's heart.

The Indians were in confusion — he could see them by the dim light, stampeding. They were running in brownish masses right around the front of the hill where he stood. He ordered the bugles to blow the charge.

The soldiers greeted the order with a yell — tired muscles, the sleepless night, its seventy-five miles of hard riding, were forgotten. The battle would be fought and won in less time than a man takes to eat his breakfast.

Down the slope swept Custer's men to meet the fleeing foe.

But now the savages had ceased to flee. They lay in the grass and fired.

Several of Custer's horses fell.

Three of his men threw up their hands, and dropped from their saddles, limp like bags of oats, and their horses ran on alone.

The gully below was full of Indians, and these sent a murderous fire at Custer as he came. His horses swerved, but several ran right on and disappeared, horse and rider in the sunken ditch, as did Napoleon's men at Waterloo.

The mad, headlong charge hesitated. The cottonwoods, the water and the teepees were a hundred yards away.

Custer glanced back, and a mile distant saw Reno's soldiers galloping wildly up the steep slope of the hill.

Reno's charge had failed — instead of riding straight down through the length of the village and meeting Custer, he had gotten only fifty rods, and then had been met by a steady fire from Indians who held their ground. He wedged them back, but his horses, already overridden, refused to go on, and the charging troops were simply carried out of the woods into the open, and once there they took to the hills for safety, leaving behind, dead, one-third of their force.

Custer quickly realized the hopelessness of charging alone into a mass of Indians, who were exultant and savage in the thought of victory. Panic was not for them.

They were armed with Springfield rifles, while the soldiers had only short-range carbines.

The bugles now ordered a retreat, and Custer's men rode back to the top of the hill — with intent to join forces with Reno.

Reno was hopelessly cut off. Determined Sioux filled the gully that separated the two little bands of brave men.

Custer, evidently, thought that Reno had simply withdrawn to re-form his troop, and that any moment Reno would ride to his rescue.

Custer decided to hold the hill.

The Indians were shooting at him from long range, occasionally killing a horse.

He told off his fours and ordered the horses sent to the rear.

The fours led their horses back toward where they had left their packmules when they had stopped for coffee at three o'clock.

But the fours had not gone half a mile when they were surrounded by a mob of Indians that just closed in on them. Every man was killed — the horses were galloped off by the women and children.

Custer now realized that he was caught in a trap. The ridge where his men lay face down was half a mile long, and not more than twenty feet across at the top. The Indians were everywhere — in the gullies, in the grass, in little scooped-out holes. The bullets whizzed above the heads of Custer's men as they lay there, flattening their bodies in the dust.

The morning sun came out, dazzling and hot.

It was only nine o'clock.

The men were without food and without water. The Little Big Horn danced over its rocky bed and shimmered in the golden light, only half a mile away, and there in the cool, limpid stream they had been confident they would now swim and fish, the battle over, while they proudly held the disarmed Indians against General Terry's coming.

But the fight had not been won, and death lay between them and water. The only thing to do was to await Reno or Terry. Reno might come at any time, and Terry would arrive without fail at tomorrow's dawn — he had said so, and his word was the word of a soldier.

Custer had blundered.

The fight was lost.

Now it was just a question of endurance. Noon came, and the buzzards began to gather in the azure.

The sun was blistering hot — there was not a tree, nor a bush, nor a green blade of grass within reach.

The men had ceased to joke and banter. The situation was serious. Some tried to smoke, but their parching thirst was thus only aggravated — they threw their pipes away.

The Indians now kept up an occasional shooting.

They were playing with the soldiers as a cat plays with a mouse.

The Indian is a cautious fighter — he makes no sacrifices in order to win. Now he had his prey secure.

Soon the soldiers would run out of ammunition, and then one more day, or two at least, and thirst and fatigue would reduce brave men into old women, and the squaws could rush in and pound them on the head with clubs.

The afternoon dragged along its awful length. Time dwindled and dawdled.

At last the sun sank, a ball of fire in the West.

The moon came out.

Now and then a Sioux would creep up into shadowy view, but a shot from a soldier would send him back into hiding. Down in the cottonwoods the squaws made campfires and were holding a dance, singing their songs of victory.

Custer warned his men that sleep was death. This was their second sleepless night, and the men were feverish with fatigue. Some babbled in strange tongues, and talked with sisters and sweethearts and people who were not there — reason was tottering.

With Custer was an Indian boy, sixteen years old, "Curley the Crow." Custer now at about midnight told Curley to strip himself and crawl out among the Indians, and if possible, get out through the lines and tell Terry of their position. Several of Custer's men had tried to reach water, but none came back.

Curley got through the lines — his boldness in mixing with the Indians and his red skin saving him. He took a long way round and ran to tell Terry the seriousness of the situation.

Terry was advancing, but was hampered and harassed by Indians for twenty miles. They fired at him from gullies, ridges, rocks, prairie-dog mounds, and then retreated. He had to move with caution. Instead of arriving at daylight as he expected, Terry was three hours behind. The Indians surrounding Custer saw the dust from the advancing troop.

They hesitated to charge Custer boldly as he lay on the hilltop, entrenched by little ditches dug in the night with knives, tin cups and bleeding fingers.

It was easy to destroy Custer, but it meant a dead Sioux for every white soldier.

The Indians made sham charges to draw Custer's fire, and then withdrew.

They circled closer. The squaws came up with sticks and stones and menaced wildly.

Custer's fire grew less and less. He was running out of ammunition.

Terry was only five miles away.

The Indians closed in like a cloud around Custer and his few survivors.

It was a hand-to-hand fight — one against a hundred.

In five minutes every man was dead, and the squaws were stripping the mangled and bleeding forms.

Already the main body of Indians was trailing across the plains toward the mountains.

Terry arrived, but it was too late.

An hour later Reno limped in, famished, half of his men dead or wounded, sick, undone.

To follow the fleeing Indians was useless — the dead soldiers must be decently buried, and the living succored. Terry himself had suffered sore.

The Indians were five thousand strong, not two. They had gathered up all the other tribes for more than a hundred miles. Now they moved North toward Canada. Terry tried to follow, but they held him off with a rear-guard, like white veterans. The Indians escaped across the border.

Anybody can order, but to serve with grace, tact and effectiveness is a fine art.

SAM

In San Francisco lived a lawyer — age, sixty — rich in money, rich in intellect, a business man with many interests.

Now, this lawyer was a bachelor, and lived in apartments with his Chinese servant "Sam."

Sam and his master had been together for fifteen years.

The servant knew the wants of his employer as though he were his other self. No orders were necessary.

If there was to be a company — one guest or a hundred — Sam was told the number, that was all, and everything was provided.

This servant was cook, valet, watchman, friend.

No stray, unwished-for visitor ever got to the master to rob him of his rest when he was at home.

If extra help was wanted, Sam secured it; he bought what was needed; and when the lawyer awakened in the morning, it was to the singing of a tiny music-box with a clock attachment set for seven o'clock.

The bath was ready; a clean shirt was there on the dresser, with studs and buttons in place; collar and scarf were near; the suit of clothes desired hung over a chair; the right pair of shoes, polished like a mirror, was at hand, and on the mantel was a half-blown rose, with the dew still upon it, for a bouton-niere.

Downstairs, the breakfast, hot and savory, waited.

When the good man was ready to go to the office, silent as a shadow stood Sam in the hallway, with overcoat, hat and cane in hand.

When the weather was threatening, an umbrella was substituted for the cane. The door was opened, and the master departed.

When he returned at nightfall, on his approach the door swung wide.

Sam never took a vacation; he seemed not to either eat or sleep.

He was always near when needed; he disappeared when he should.

He knew nothing and he knew everything.

For weeks scarcely a word might pass between these men, they understood each other so well.

The lawyer grew to have a great affection for his servant.

He paid him a hundred dollars a month, and tried to devise other ways to show his gratitude; but Sam wanted nothing, not even thanks.

All he desired was the privilege to serve.

But one morning as Sam poured his master's coffee, he said quietly, without a shade of emotion on his yellow face, "Next week I leave you."

The lawyer smiled.

"Next week I leave you," repeated the Chinese; "I hire for you better man."

The lawyer set down his cup of coffee. He looked at the white-robed servant. He felt the man was in earnest.

"So you are going to leave me — I do not pay you enough, eh? That Doctor Sanders who was here — he knows what a treasure you are. Don't be a fool, Sam; I'll make it a hundred and fifty a month — say no more."

"Next week I leave you — I go to China," said the servant impassively.

"Oh, I see! You are going back for a wife? All right, bring her here — you will return in two months? I do not object; bring your wife here — there is work for two to keep this place in order. The place is lonely, anyway. I'll see the Collector of the Port, myself, and arrange your passage-papers."

"I go to China next week: I need no papers — I never come back," said the man with exasperating calmness and persistence.

"By God, you shall not go!" said the lawyer.

"By God, I will!" answered the heathen.

It was the first time in their experience together that the servant had used such language, or such a tone, toward his master.

The lawyer pushed his chair back, and after an instant said, quietly, "Sam, you must forgive me; I spoke quickly. I do not own you — but tell me, what have I done — why do you leave me this way, you know I need you!"

"I will not tell you why I go — you laugh."

"No, I shall not laugh."

"You will."

"I say, I will not."

"Very well, I go to China to die!"

"Nonsense! You can die here. Haven't I agreed to send your body back if you die before I do?"

"I die in four weeks, two days!"

"What!"

"My brother, he in prison. He twenty-six, I fifty. He have wife and baby. In China they accept any man same family to die. I go to China, give my money to my brother — he live, I die!"

The next day a new Chinaman appeared as servant in the lawyer's household. In a week this servant knew everything, and nothing, just like Sam.

And Sam disappeared, without saying good-by.

He went to China and was beheaded, four weeks and two days from the day he broke the news of his intent to go.

His brother was set free.

And the lawyer's household goes along about as usual, save when the master calls for "Sam," when he should say, "Charlie."

At such times there comes a kind of clutch at his heart, but he says nothing.

When power and beauty meet, the world would do well to take to its cyclone-cellar.

CLEOPATRA
AND CÆSAR

The sole surviving daughter of the great King Ptolemy of Egypt, Cleopatra was seventeen years old when her father died.

By his will the King made her joint heir to the throne with her brother Ptolemy, several years her junior. And according to the custom not unusual among royalty at that time, it was provided that Ptolemy should become the husband of Cleopatra.

She was a woman — her brother a child.

She had intellect, ambition, talent. She knew the history of her own country, and that of Assyria, Greece and Rome; and all the written languages of the world were to her familiar. She had been educated by the philosophers, who had brought from Greece the science of Pythagoras and Plato. Her companions had been men — not women, or nurses, or pious, pedantic priests.

Through the veins of her young body pulsed and leaped life, plus.

She abhorred the thought of an alliance with her

weak-chinned brother; and the ministers of State, who suggested another husband as a compromise, were dismissed with a look.

They said she was intractable, contemptuous, unreasonable, and was scheming for the sole possession of the throne.

She was not to be diverted even by ardent courtiers who were sent to her, and who lay in wait ready with amorous sighs — she scorned them all.

Yet she was a woman still, and in her dreams she saw the coming prince.

She was banished from Alexandria.

A few friends followed her, and an army was formed to force from the enemy her rights.

But other things were happening — a Roman army came leisurely drifting in with the tide and disembarked at Alexandria. The Great Cæsar himself was in command — a mere holiday, he said. He had intended to join the land forces of Mark Antony and help crush the rebellious Pompey, but Antony had done the trick alone; and only a few days before, word had come that Pompey was dead.

Cæsar knew that civil war was on in Alexandria, and being near he sailed slowly in, sending messengers on ahead warning both sides to lay down their arms.

With him was the far-famed invincible Tenth Legion that had ravished Gaul. Cæsar wanted to rest his men and, incidentally, to reward them. They took possession of the city without a blow.

Cleopatra's troops laid down their arms, but Ptolemy's refused. They were simply chased beyond the walls, and their punishment for the time being was deferred.

Cæsar took possession of the palace of the King, and his soldiers accommodated themselves in the houses, public buildings, and temples as best they could.

Cleopatra asked for a personal interview, in order to present her cause.

Cæsar declined to meet her — he understood the trouble — many such cases he had seen. Claimants for thrones were not new to him. Where two parties quarreled, both are right — or wrong — it really mattered little.

It is absurd to quarrel — still more foolish to fight.

Cæsar was a man of peace, and to keep the peace he would appoint one of his generals governor, and make Egypt a Roman colony.

In the meantime he would rest a week or two, with the kind permission of the Alexandrians, and write upon his "Commentaries" — no, he would not see either Cleopatra or Ptolemy — any desired information they would get through his trusted emissaries.

In the service of Cleopatra was a Sicilian slave who had been her personal servant since she was a little girl. This man's name was Appolidorus. He was a man of giant stature and imposing mien. Ten years before his tongue had been torn out as a token that as he was to attend a queen he should tell no secrets.

Appolidorus had but one thought in life, and

that was to defend his gracious queen. He slept at the door of Cleopatra's tent, a naked sword at his side, held in his clenched and brawny hand.

And now behold at dusk of day the grim and silent Appolidorus, carrying upon his giant shoulders a large and curious rug, rolled up and tied 'round at each end with ropes.

He approaches the palace of the King, and at the guarded gate hands a note to the officer in charge. This note gives information to the effect that a certain patrician citizen of Alexandria, being glad that the gracious Cæsar had deigned to visit Egypt, sends him the richest rug that can be woven — done, in fact, by his wife and daughters and held against this day, awaiting Rome's greatest son.

The officer reads the note, and orders a soldier to accept the gift and carry it within — presents were constantly arriving. A sign from the dumb giant makes the soldier stand back — the present is for Cæsar and can be delivered only in person. "Lead and I will follow," were the words done in stern pantomime. The officer laughs, sends in the note, and the messenger soon returning, signifies that the present is acceptable and the slave bearing it shall be shown in. Appolidorus shifts his burden to the other shoulder, and follows the soldier through the gate, up the marble steps, along the splendid hallway, lighted by flaring torches and lined with reclining Roman soldiers.

At a door they pause an instant, there is a whispered word — they enter.

The room is furnished as becomes the room that

is the private library of the King of Egypt. In one corner, seated at the table, pen in hand, sits a man of middle age, pale, clean-shaven, with hair close-cropped. His dress is not that of a soldier — it is the flowing white robe of a Roman Priest. Only one servant attends this man, a secretary, seated near, who rises and explains that the present is acceptable and shall be deposited on the floor.

The pale man at the table looks up, smiles a tired smile and murmurs in a perfunctory way his thanks.

Appolidorus having laid his burden on the floor, kneels to untie the ropes. The secretary explains that he need not trouble, pray bear thanks and again thanks to his master — he need not tarry!

The dumb man on his knees neither hears nor heeds. The rug is unrolled.

From out the roll a woman leaps lightly to her feet — a beautiful young woman of twenty.

She stands there, poised, defiant, gazing at the pale-faced man seated at the table.

He is not surprised — he never was. One might have supposed he received all his visitors in this manner.

"Well?" he says in a quiet way, a half-smile parting his thin lips.

The breast of the woman heaves with tumultuous emotion — just an instant. She speaks, and there is no tremor in her tones. Her voice is low, smooth and scarcely audible: "I am Cleopatra."

The man at the desk lays down his pen, leans back and gently nods his head, as much as to say, indulgently, "Yes, my child, I hear — go on!"

"I am Cleopatra, Queen of Egypt, and I would speak with thee, alone."

She pauses; then raising one jeweled arm motions to Appolidorus that he shall withdraw.

With a similar motion, the man at the desk signifies the same to his astonished secretary.

Appolidorus went down the long hallway, down the stone steps and waited at the outer gate amid the throng of soldiers. They questioned him, gibed him, railed at him, but they got no word in reply.

He waited — he waited an hour, two — and then came a messenger with a note written on a slip of parchment. The words ran thus: "Well-beloved 'Dorus: Veni, vidi, vici! Go fetch my maids; also, all of our personal belongings."

As the cities are all only two days from famine, so is man's life constantly but a step from dissolution.

A SPECIAL OCCASION

Once on a day, I spoke at the Athenæum, New Orleans, for the Young Men's Hebrew Association.

When they had asked my fee I answered, "One Hundred Fifty Dollars." The reply was, "We will pay you Two Hundred — it is to be a special occasion."

A carriage was sent to my hotel for me. The Jews may be close traders, but when it comes to social functions, they know what to do. The Jew is the most generous man in the world, even if he can be at times cent per cent.

As I approached the Athenæum I thought, "What a beautiful building!" It was stone and brick — solid, subdued, complete and substantial. The lower rooms were used for the Hebrew Club. Upstairs stretched the splendid hall, as I could tell from the brilliantly lighted windows.

Inside, I noticed that the stairways were carpeted with Brussels. Glancing through the wide doorways, I beheld an audience of more than two thousand people. The great chandeliers sent out a dazzling glory from their crystal and gold. At the sides, rich tapestries and hangings of velvet covered the windows.

"A beautiful building," I said to my old-time friend, Maurice J. Pass, the Secretary of the Club.

He smiled in satisfaction and replied, "Well, we seldom let things go by default — you have tonight as fine an audience as ever assembled in New Orleans."

We passed down a side hallway and under the stage, preparatory to going on the platform. In this room below the stage a single electric light shone. The place was dark and dingy, in singular contrast to the beauty, light, cleanliness and order just beyond. In the corner were tables piled high — evidently used for banquets — broken furniture and discarded boxes.

Several smart young men in full dress sat on the tables smoking cigarettes. One young man said in explanation, "We were crowded out — had to give up our seats to ladies — so we are going to sit on the stage."

The soft blue smoke from the cigarettes seemed to hug close about the lonely electric light.

I saw the smoke and thought that beside the odor of tobacco I detected the smell of smoldering pine.

"Isn't it a trifle smoky here?" I said to the young man nearest me.

He laughed at this remark and handed me a cigarette.

The Secretary of the Club and I went up the narrow stairs to the stage. As we stood there behind the curtain I looked at the pleasant-faced man. "You didn't detect the odor of burning wood down there, did you?" I asked.

"No; but you see the windows are open, and there are bonfires outside, I suppose."

"I am a fool," I thought; "and James Whitcomb Riley was right when he said that the speaker who is about to make his bow to an audience is always so keyed up that at the moment he is incapable of sane thinking."

I excused myself and walked over to an open window at the back of the stage and looked down.

It must have been forty feet to the stony street beneath.

Then I went to a side window and threw up the sash. This window looked out on a roof ten or twelve feet below. I got a broken broom that stood in the corner and propped the window open.

The thought of fire was upon me and I was inwardly planning what I would do in case of a stampede. I am always thinking about what I would do should this or that happen. Nothing can surprise me — not even death. If any of my best helpers should leave me, I have it all planned exactly whom I will put in their places. I have it arranged who will take my own place — my will is made and my body is to be cremated.

"Cremated? Not tonight!" I said to myself, as I placed the broom under the sash. "If a panic occurs, the people will go out of the doors and I will stick to the stage until my coat-tails singe. I'll say that the fire is in an adjoining building; then I'll smilingly bow myself off the stage and gently drop out of that window."

"All ready when you are," said Mr. Fass.

I passed out on the stage before that vast sea of faces.

It was a glorious sight. There was a row of military men from the French warship in the harbor, down in front; priests, and ladies with sparkling diamonds; a bishop wearing a purple vestment under his black gown sat to one side; a stout lady in décolleté waved a feather fan in rhythmic, mystic motion, far back to the left.

The audience applauded encouragingly, I wished I was back in that dear East Aurora. But I began.

In a few minutes my heart ceased to thump and I knew we were off.

I spoke for two hours, and I spoke well.

I did not push the lecture in front of me, nor did I drag it behind. I got the chancery twist on it and carried it off big, as I do about one time in ten. I finished in a whirlwind of applause, with the bishop crying "Bravo!" and the fat lady with the fifty-dollar feather fan beaming approbation.

Fass stood in the wings to congratulate me.

I shook hands with a hundred. The house slowly emptied. I bade the genial Fass good-by. He took my hand in both of his. "You will come back! You must come back!" he said.

He walked with me, bareheaded, to my carriage.

He again pressed my hand.

I rode to my hotel and went to bed, and to sleep.

I was awakened by a bright glare of light that filled my room.

I got up and looked at my watch. It was just midnight.

Off to the East I saw red tongues of angry flame streaking the sky from horizon to zenith.

"It is the Jewish Club, all right," I said.

I pulled down the blind and went back to bed.

When I went down to breakfast at seven o'clock in the morning, I heard the newsboys in the streets crying, "All about the fire!" I bought a paper and read the headline, "Hubbard's Lecture Hot Stuff!"

I walked out Saint Charles Avenue and viewed the smoldering ruins where only a few hours before I had spoken to more than two thousand people — where the bishop in purple vestment had cried "Bravo!" and the stout lady with feathered fan had beamed approval.

"Was anybody hurt?" I asked one of the policemen on guard.

"Only one man killed — Fass, the Secretary; I believe he lies somewhere over there to the left, beneath that toppled wall."

The person who reasons from a false premise is always funny — to other folks.

UNCLE JOE AND AUNT MELINDA

The opinion prevails all through the truly rural districts that the big cities are for the most part given over to Confidence Men.

And the strange part is that the opinion is correct.

But it should not be assumed that all the people in, say, Buffalo, are moral derelicts — there are many visitors there, most of the time, from other sections.

And while at all times one should exercise caution, yet to assume that the party who is "fresh" is intent on high crimes and misdemeanors may be a rather hasty and unjust generalization.

For instance, there are Uncle Joe and Aunt Melinda, who live eight miles back from East Aurora, at Wales Hollow. They had been married for forty-seven years, and had never taken a wedding journey. They decided to go to Buffalo and spend two days at a hotel regardless of expense.

Much had been told them about the Confidence Men who hang around the railroad-station, and they were prepared.

They arrived at East Aurora, where they were to take the train, an hour ahead of time. The Jerkwater came in and they were duly seated, when all at once Uncle Joe rushed for the door, jumped off and made for the waiting-room looking for his carpetbag. It was on the train all right, but he just forgot, and feeling sure he had left it in the station made the grand skirmish as aforesaid.

The result was that the train went off and left your Uncle Joseph.

Aunt Melinda was much exercised, but the train-hands pacified her by assurances that her husband would follow on the next train, and she should simply wait for him in the depot at Buffalo.

Now the Flyer was right behind the Jerkwater, and Uncle Joe took the Flyer and got to Buffalo first. When the Jerkwater came in, Uncle Joe was on the platform waiting for Aunt Melinda.

As she disembarked he approached her.

She shied and passed on.

He persisted in his attentions.

Then it was that she shook her umbrella at him and bade him hike. The eternally feminine in her nature prompted self-preservation. She banked on her reason — woman's reason — not her intuition. She had started first — her husband could only come on a later train.

"Go 'way and leave me alone," she shouted in shrill falsetto. "You have got yourself up to look like my Joe — and that idiotic grin on your homely face is just like my Joe, but no city sharper can fool me, and if you don't go right along I'll call for the perlice!"

She called for the police, and Uncle Joe had to show a strawberry-mark to prove his identity, before he received recognition.

To be your brother's keeper is beautiful if you do not cease to be his friend.

BILLY AND THE BOOK

One day last Winter in New York I attended a police court on a side street, just off lower Broadway. I was waiting to see my old friend Rosenfeld in the Equitable Life Building, but as his office didn't open up until nine o'clock, I put in my time at the police court.

There was the usual assortment of drunks, petty thieves — male and female, black, white and coffee-colored — disorderlies, vagabonds and a man in full-dress suit and a wide expanse of dull ecru shirt-bosom.

The place was stuffy, foul-smelling, and reeked with a stale combination of tobacco and beer and patchouli, and tears, curses, fear and promises un-kept.

The Judge turned things off, but without haste. He showed more patience and consideration than one usually sees on the bench. His judgments seemed to be gentle and just.

The courtroom was clearing, and I started to go.

As I was passing down the icy steps a piping child's voice called to me, "Mister, please give me a lift!"

There at the foot of the steps, standing in the snow, was a slender slip of a girl, yellow and earnest, say ten years old, with a shawl pinned over her head. She held in her hand a rope, and this rope was tied to a hand-sled. On this sled sat a little boy, shivering, dumpy and depressed, his bare red hands clutching the seat.

"Mister, I say, please give me a lift!"

"Sure!" I said.

It was a funny sight.

This girl seemed absolutely unconscious of herself. She was not at all abashed, and very much in earnest about something.

Evidently she had watched the people coming out and had waited until one appeared that she thought safe to call on for help.

"Of course I'll give you a lift — what is it you want me to do?"

"I've got to go inside and see the Judge. It's about my brudder here. He is six, goin' on seven, and they sent him home from school 'cause they said he wasn't old enough. I'm going to have that teacher 'rested. I've got the Bible here that says he's six years old. If you'll carry the book I'll bring Billy and the sled!"

"Where is the Bible?" I asked.

"Billy's settin' on it."

It was a big, black, greasy Family Bible, evidently a relic of better days. It had probably been hidden under the bed for safety.

The girl grappled the sled with one hand, and with the other Billy's little red fist.

I followed, carrying the big, black, greasy Family Bible.

Evidently this girl had been here before. She walked around the end of the judicial bar, and laid down the sled. Then she took the Bible out of my hands. It was about all she could do to lift it.

In a shrill, piping voice, full of business, and very much in earnest, she addressed the Judge: "I say, Mister Judge, they sent my brudder Billy away from school, they did. He's six, goin' on seven, and I want that teacher 'rested and brought here so you can tell her to let Billy go to school. Here is our Family Bible — you can see for yourself how old Billy is!"

The Judge adjusted his glasses, stared, and exclaimed, "God bless my soul!"

Then he called a big, blue-coated officer over and said: "Mike, you go with this little girl and her brother, and tell that teacher, if possible, to allow the boy to go to school; that I say he is old enough. You understand! If you do not succeed, come back and tell me why."

The officer smiled and saluted.

The big policeman took the little boy in his arms. The girl carried the sled, and I followed with the Family Bible.

The officer looked at me — "Newspaper man, I s'pose?"

"Yes," I said.

"What paper?"

"The American."

"It's the best ever."

"I think so — possibly with a few exceptions."

"She's the queerest lot yet, is this kid," and the big bluecoat jerked his thumb toward the girl.

I suggested that we go to the restaurant across the way and get a bite of something to eat.

"I'm not hungry," said the officer, "but the youngsters look as if they hadn't et since day before yesterday."

We lined up at the counter.

The officer drank two cups of coffee and ate a ham sandwich, two hard-boiled eggs, a plate of cakes and a piece of pie.

The girl and her brother each had a plate of cakes, a piece of pie and a glass of milk.

"What's yours?" asked the waiter.

"Same," said I.

As I did not care for the cakes, the officer cleaned the plate for me.

I didn't have time to go to the school, but the officer assured me that he would "fix it," and he winked knowingly, as if he had looked after such things before. He was kind, but determined, and I had confidence he would see that the little boy was duly admitted.

I started up the street alone.

They went the other way. The officer carried the little boy.

The girl with the shawl over her head followed, pulling the hand-sled, and on the sled rested the big, black Family Bible. I lost sight of them as they turned the corner.

An act is only a crystallized thought.

JOHN THE BAPTIST AND SALOME

John the Baptist, the strong, fine youth, came up out of the wilderness crying in the streets of Jerusalem, "Repent ye! Repent ye!"

Salome heard the call and from her window looked with half-closed, catlike eyes upon the semi-naked, young fanatic.

She smiled, did this idle creature of luxury, as she lay there amid the cushions on her couch, and gazed through the casement upon the preacher in the street.

Suddenly a thought came to her.

She arose on her elbow — she called her slaves.

They clothed her in a gaudy gown, dressed her hair, and led her forth.

Salome followed the wild, weird, religious enthusiast.

She pushed through the crowd and placed herself near the man, so the smell of her body would reach his nostrils.

His eyes ranged the swelling lines of her body.

Their eyes met.

She half-smiled and gave him that look which had snared the soul of many another.

But he only gazed at her with passionless, judging intensity and repeated his cry, "Repent ye. Repent ye, for the day is at hand!"

Her reply, uttered soft and low, was this: "I would kiss thy lips!"

He moved away and she reached to seize his garment, repeating, "I would kiss thy lips — I would kiss thy lips!"

He turned aside, and forgot her, as he continued his warning cry, and went his way.

The next day she waylaid the youth again; as he came near she suddenly and softly stepped forth and said in that same low, purring voice, "I would kiss thy lips!"

He repulsed her with scorn.

She threw her arms about him and sought to draw his head down near hers.

He pushed her from him with sinewy hands, sprang as from a pestilence, and was lost in the pressing throng.

That night she danced before Herod Antipas, and when the promise was recalled that she should have anything she wished, she named the head of the only man who had ever turned away from her. "The head of John the Baptist on a charger!"

In an hour the wish was gratified.

Two eunuchs stood before Salome with a silver tray bearing its fearsome burden.

The woman smiled — a smile of triumph, as she

stepped forth with tinkling feet.

A look of pride came over the painted face.

Her jeweled fingers reached into the blood-matted hair. She lifted the head aloft, and the bracelets on her brown, bare arms fell to her shoulders, making strange music. Her face pressed the face of the dead.

In exultation she exclaimed, "I have kissed thy lips!"

He who influences the thought of his time influences the thought of all the time that follows. And he has made his impress upon eternity.

THE MASTER

Giovanni Bellini was his name.

Yet when people who loved beautiful pictures spoke of "Gian," every one knew who was meant; but to those who worked at art he was "The Master." He was two inches under six feet in height, strong and muscular. In spite of his seventy summers his carriage was erect, and there was a jaunty suppleness about his gait that made him seem much younger. In fact, no one would have believed he had lived over his threescore and ten, were it not for the iron-gray hair that fluffed out all around under the close-fitting black cap, and the bronzed complexion — sun-kissed by wind and by weather — which formed a trinity of opposites that made people turn and stare.

Queer stories used to be told about him. He was a skilful gondolier, and it was the daily row back and forth from the Lido that gave him that face of bronze. Folks said he ate no meat and drank no wine, and that his food was simply ripe figs in the season, with coarse rye bread and nuts.

Then there was that funny old hunchback, a hundred years old at least, and stone-deaf, who took care of the gondola, spending the whole day, waiting for his master, washing the trim, graceful, blue-black boat, arranging the awning with the white cords and tassels, and polishing the little brass lions at the sides. People tried to question the old hunchback, but he gave no secrets away. The master always stood up behind and rowed; while down on the cushions rode the hunchback, the guest of honor.

There stood the master erect, plying the oar, his long black robe tucked up under the dark blue sash that exactly matched the color of the gondola. The man's motto might have been, "Ich Dien," or that passage of Scripture, "He that is greatest among you shall be your servant." Suspended around his neck by a slender chain was a bronze medal, presented by vote of the Signoria when the great picture of "The Transfiguration" was unveiled. If this medal had been a crucifix, and you had met the wearer in San Marco, one glance at the finely chiseled features, the black cap and the flowing robe and you would have said at once the man was a priest, Vicar-General of some important diocese. But seeing him standing erect on the stern of a gondola, the wind caressing the dark gray hair, you would have been perplexed until your gondolier explained in serious undertone that you had just passed "the greatest Painter in all Venice, Gian, the Master."

Then, if you showed curiosity and wanted to know further, the gondolier would have told you more about this strange man.

The canals of Venice are the highways, and the gondoliers are like 'bus-drivers in Piccadilly — they know everybody and are in close touch with all the Secrets of State. When you get to the Gindecca and tie up for lunch, over a bottle of Chianti, your gondolier will tell you this:

The hunchback there in the gondola, rowed by the Master, is the Devil, who has taken that form just to be with and guard the greatest artist the world has ever seen. Yes, Signor, that clean-faced man with his frank, wide-open, brown eyes is in league with the Evil One. He is the man who took young Tiziano from Cadore into his shop, right out of a glass-factory, and made him a great artist, getting him commissions and introducing him everywhere! And how about the divine Giorgione who called him father? Oho!

And who is Giorgione? The son of some unknown peasant woman. And if Bellini wanted to adopt him, treat him as his son indeed, kissing him on the cheek when he came back just from a day's visit to Mestre, whose business was it! Oho!

Beside that, his name isn't Giorgione — it is Giorgio Barbarelli. And didn't this Giorgio Barbarelli, and Tiziano from Cadore, and Espero Carbonne, and that Gustavo from Nuremberg, and the others paint most of Gian's pictures? Surely they did. The old man simply washes in the backgrounds and the boys do the work. About all old Gian does is to sign the picture, sell it and pocket the proceeds. Carpaccio helps him, too — Carpaccio who painted the loveliest little angel sitting cross-legged playing the biggest mandolin you ever saw in your life.

That is genius, you know, the ability to get some one else to do the work, and then capture the ducats and the honors for yourself. Of course, Gian knows how to lure the boys on — something has to be done in order to hold them. Gian buys a picture from them now and then; his studio is full of their work — better than he can do. Oh, he knows a good thing when he sees it. These pictures will be valuable some day, and he gets them at his own price. It was Antonello of Messina who introduced oil-painting into Venice. Before that they mixed their paints with water, milk or wine. But when Antonello came along with his dark, lustrous pictures, he set all artistic Venice astir. Gian Bellini discovered the secret, they say, by feigning to be a gentleman and going to the newcomer and sitting for his picture. He it was who discovered that Antonello mixed his colors with oil. Oho!

Of course, not all of the pictures in his studio are painted by the boys: some are painted by that old Dutchman what's-his-name — oh, yes, Durer, Alberto Durer of Nuremberg. Two Nuremberg painters were in that very gondola last week just where you sit — they are here in Venice now, taking lessons from Gian, they said. Gian was up there to Nuremberg and lived a month with Durer — they worked together, drank beer together, I suppose, and caroused. Gian is very strict about what he does in Venice, but you can never tell what a man will do when he is away from home. The Germans are a roystering lot — but they do say they can paint. Me?

I have never been up there — and do not want to go, either — there are no canals there. To be sure, they print books in Nuremberg. It was up there somewhere that they invented type, a lazy scheme to do away with writing. They are a thrifty lot — those Germans — they give me my fare and a penny more, just a single penny, and no matter how much I have talked and pointed out the wonderful sights, and imparted useful information, known to me alone — only one penny extra — think of it!

Yes, printing was first done at Mayence by a German, Gutenberg, about sixty years ago. One of Gutenberg's workmen went up to Nuremberg and taught others how to design and cast type. This man, Alberto Durer, helped them, designing the initials and making their title-pages by cutting the design on a wood block, then covering this block with ink, laying a sheet of paper upon it, placing it in a press, and then when the paper is lifted off it looks exactly like the original drawing. In fact, most people couldn't tell the difference, and here you can print thousands of them from the one block.

Bellini makes drawings for title-pages and initials for Aldus and Nicholas Jenson. Venice is the greatest printing place in the world, and yet the business began here only thirty years ago. The first book printed here was in Fourteen Hundred Sixty-nine, by John of Speyer. There are two hundred licensed printing-presses here, and it takes usually four men to a press — two to set the type and get things ready, and two to run the press. This does not count, of course, the men who write the books, and those who make the type and cut the blocks from which they print the pictures for the illustrations. At first, you know, the books they printed in Venice had no title-pages, initials or illustrations. My father was a printer and he remembers when the first large initials were printed — before that the spaces were left blank and the books were sent out to the monasteries to be completed by hand.

Gian and Gentile had a good deal to do about cutting the first blocks for initials — they got the idea, I think, from Nuremberg. And now there are Dutchmen down here from Amsterdam learning how to print books and paint pictures. Several of them are in Gian's studio, I hear — every once in a while I get them for a trip to the Lido or to Murano.

Gentile Bellini is his brother and looks very much like him. The Grand Turk at Constantinople came here once and saw Gian Bellini at work in the Great Hall. He had never seen a good picture before and was amazed. He wanted the Senate to sell Gian to him, thinking he was a slave. They humored the Pagan by hiring Gentile Bellini to go instead, loaning him out for two years, so to speak.

Gentile went, and the Sultan, who never allowed any one to stand before him, all having to grovel in the dirt, treated Gentile as an equal. Gentile even taught the old rogue to draw a little, and they say the painter had a key to every room in the palace, and was treated like a prince.

Well, they got along all right, until one day Gentile drew the picture of the head of John the Baptist on a charger.

"A man's head doesn't look like that when it is cut off," said the Grand Turk contemptuously. Gentile had forgotten that the Turk was on familiar ground.

"Perhaps the Light of the Sun knows more about painting than I do!" said Gentile, as he kept right on at his work.

"I may not know much about painting, but I'm no fool in some other things I might name," was the reply.

The Sultan clapped his hands three times: two slaves appeared from opposite doors. One was a little ahead of the other, and as this one approached, the Sultan with a single swing of the snickersnee snipped off his head. This teaches us that obedience to our superiors is its own reward. But the lesson was wholly lost on Gentile Bellini, for he did not even remain to examine the severed head for art's sake. The thought that it might be his turn next was supreme, and he leaped through a window, taking the sash with him. Making his way to the docks he found a sailing vessel loading with fruit, bound for Venice. A small purse of gold made the matter easy: the captain of the boat secreted him, and in four days he was safely back in Saint Mark's giving thanks to God for his deliverance.

No, I didn't say Gian was a rogue — I only told you what others say. I am only a poor gondolier — why should I trouble myself about what great folks do? I simply tell you what I hear — it may be so, and it may not. God knows! There is that Pascale Salvini — he has a rival studio — and when that

Genoese, Christoforo Colombo, was here and made his stopping-place at Bellini's studio, Pascale told every one that Colombo was a lunatic, and Bellini another, for encouraging him to show his foolish maps and charts. Now, they do say that Colombo has discovered a new world, and Italians are feeling troubled in conscience because they did not fit him out with ships instead of forcing him to go to Spain.

No, I didn't say Bellini was a hypocrite — Pascale's pupils say so, and once they followed him over to Murano — three barca-loads and my gondola beside. You see it was like this: Twice a week just after sundown, we used to see Gian Bellini untie his boat from the landing there behind the Doge's palace, turn the prow, and beat out for Murano, with no companion but that deaf old caretaker. Twice a week, Tuesdays and Fridays — always at just the same hour, regardless of the weather — we would see the old hunchback light the lamps, and in a few moments the Master would appear, tuck up his black robe, step into the boat, take the oar and away they would go. It was always to Murano, and always to the same landing — one of our gondoliers had followed them several times, just out of curiosity.

Finally it came to the ears of Pascale that Gian took this regular trip to Murano. "It is a rendez-vous," said Pascale. "It is worse than that: an orgy among those lacemakers and the rogues of the glass-works. Oh, to think that Gian should stoop to such things at his age — his pretended asceticism is but a mask — and at his age!"

The Pascale students took it up, and once came

in collision with that Tiziano of Cadore, who they say broke a boat-hook over the head of one of them who had spoken ill of the Master.

But this did not silence the talk, and one dark night, when the air was full of flying mist, one of Pascale's students came to me and told me that he wanted me to take a party over to Murano. The weather was so bad that I refused to go — the wind blew in gusts, sheet lightning filled the Eastern sky, and all honest men, but poor belated gondoliers, had hied them home.

I refused to go.

Had I not seen Gian the painter go not half an hour before? Well, if he could go, others could too.

I refused to go — except for double fare.

He accepted and placed the double fare in silver in my palm. Then he gave a whistle and from behind the corners came trooping enough swashbuckler students to swamp my gondola. I let in just enough to fill the seats and pushed off, leaving several standing on the stone steps cursing me and everything and everybody.

As my boat slid away in the fog and headed on our course, I glanced back and saw the three barca-loads following in my wake.

There was much muffled talk, and orders from some one in charge to keep silence. But there was passing of strong drink, and then talk, and from it I gathered that these were all students from Pascale's, out on one of those student carousals, intent on heaven knows what! It was none of my business.

We shipped considerable water, and some of the

students were down on their knees praying and bail-ing, bailing and praying.

At last we reached the Murano landing. All got out, the barcas tied up, and I tied up, too, deter-mined to see what was doing. The strong drink was passed, and a low, heavy-set fellow who seemed to be captain charged all not to speak, but to follow him and do as he did.

We took a side street where there was little travel and followed through the dark and dripping way, fully a half-mile, down there in that end of the island called the sailors' broglio, where they say no man's life is safe if he has a silver coin or two. There was much music in the wine-shops and shouts of mirth and dancing feet on stone floors, but the rain had driven every one from the streets.

We came to a long, low, stone building that used to be a theater, but was now a dance-hall upstairs and a warehouse below. There were lights upstairs and sounds of music. The stairway was dark, but we felt our way up and on tiptoe advanced to the big double door, from under which the light streamed.

We had received our orders, and when we got to the landing we stood there just an instant. "Now we have him — Gian the hypocrite!" whispered the stout man in a hoarse breath. We burst in the doors with a whoop and a bang. The change from the dark to the light sort of blinded us at first. We all sup-posed that there was a dance in progress of course, and the screams from women were just what we expected; but when we saw several overturned easels and an old man, half-nude, and too scared to move, seated on a model throne, we did not advance into the hall as we intended. That one yell we gave was all the noise we made. We stood there in a bunch, just inside the door, sort of dazed and uncertain. We did not know whether to retreat, or charge on through the hall as we had intended. We just stood there like a lot of driveling fools.

"Keep right at your work, my good people. Keep right at your work!" called a pleasant voice. "I see we have some visitors."

And Gian Bellini came forward. His robe was still tucked up under the blue sash, but he had laid aside his black cap, and his tumbled gray hair looked like the aureole of a saint. "Keep right at your work," he said again, and then came forward and bade us welcome and begged us to have seats.

I dared not run away, so I sat down on one of the long seats that were ranged around the wall. My companions did the same. There must have been fifty easels, all ranged in a semicircle around the old man who posed as a model. Several of the easels had been upset, and there was much confusion when we entered.

"Just help us to arrange things — that is right, thank you," said Gian to the stout man who was captain of our party. To my astonishment the stout man was doing just as he was bid, and was pacifying the women students and straightening up their easels and stools.

I was interested in watching Gian walking around, helping this one with a stroke of his crayon, saying a word to that, smiling and nodding to another. I just sat there and stared. These students were not regular art students, I could see that plainly. Some were children, ragged and barelegged, others were old men who worked in the glass-factories, and surely with hands too old and stiff to ever paint well. Still others were women and young girls of the town. I rubbed my eyes and tried to make it out!

The music we heard I could still hear — it came from the wine-shop across the way. I looked around and what do you believe? My companions had all gone. They had sneaked out one by one and left me alone.

I watched my chance and when the Master's back was turned I tiptoed out, too.

When I got down on the street I found I had left my cap, but I dared not go back after it. I made my way down to the landing, half running, and when I got there not a boat was to be seen — the three barcas and my gondola were gone.

I thought I could see them, out through the mist, a quarter of a mile away. I called aloud, but no answer came back but the hissing wind. I was in despair — they were stealing my boat, and if they did not steal it, it would surely be wrecked — my all, my precious boat!

I cried and wrung my hands. I prayed! And the howling winds only ran shrieking and laughing around the corners of the building.

I saw a glimmering light down the beach at a little landing. I ran to it, hoping some gondolier might be found who would row me over to the city. There was one boat at the landing and in it a hunchback, sound asleep, covered with a canvas. It was Gian Bellini's boat. I shook the hunchback into wakefulness and begged him to row me across to the city. I yelled into his deaf ears, but he pretended not to understand me. Then I showed him the silver coin — the double fare — and tried to place it in his hand. But no, he only shook his head.

I ran up the beach, still looking for a boat.

An hour had passed.

I got back to the landing just as Gian came down to his boat.

I approached him and explained that I was a poor worker in the glass-factory, who had to work all day and half the night, and as I lived over in the city and my wife was dying, I must get home. Would he allow me to ride with His Highness? "Certainly — with pleasure, with pleasure!" he answered, and then pulling something from under his sash he said, "Is this your cap, Signor?" I took my cap, but my tongue was paralyzed for the moment so I could not thank him.

The wind had died down, the rain had ceased, and from between the blue-black clouds the moon shone out. Gian rowed with a strong, fine stroke, singing a "Te Deum Laudamus" softly to himself the while.

I lay there and wept, thinking of my boat, my all, my precious boat!

We reached the landing — and there was my

boat, safely tied up, not a cushion nor a cord missing.

Gian Bellini? He may be a rogue as Pascale Salvini says — God knows! How can I tell — I am only a poor gondolier!